# BALANCE OF RETRIBUTION

by Paul Heingarten

Published by Decatur Media
New Orleans, Louisiana
www.decaturmedia.com

ISBN: # 978-1-960028-05-1

Cover design by Y. Nikolova at Ammonia Book Covers

## Acknowledgements

First and foremost, thank you to my wife Andrea, thank you for loving me and for your endless support, I couldn't do this without you.

To my family, for endless love, support, and encouragement.

To Lisa Herrington, thank you once again for your friendship and pep talks!

To Jenny Bodle, I'm so glad we met. You've gone beyond being a PA and I consider you a good friend. Looking forward to collaborating with you in the future.

To Carissa Andrews, for being such a beacon of positivity and support, and for taking time to interact with me amid my endless series of questions.

To the Bayou Writers Club. Thank you for hours of discussions about writing, the camaraderie, and for your support.

Special thanks to my street team, the "Krewe of Paul" for helping me become the best writer I can. Find out about the Krewe of Paul and get free books at my site www.paulheingarten.com

*For Andrea, with all my love*

# Chapter 1

"WHAT'S YOUR NEWS?"

Findlay Mantisword handled questions far more involved than that on a daily basis. In his position as Chief of Scientific Development for the Omegans, his nerves endured a consistent test every day, from Emperor Zakmar down to the science staff under his lead. He handled things as well as one in a position like his could, but even Omegans had their occasional outbursts when the benign or ridiculous was too much to handle with a simple shrug of the shoulders.

But this time, it wasn't as easy. It wasn't the nature of the question so much as it was who asked it. "You're dying to know what it is, aren't you, Charista?" he smiled.

Charista wrapped her arms around the back of her chair. "Come on, Dad, you can't build something like this up and keep me waiting."

Findlay chuckled. "Alright, alright." He grabbed a seat next to her and stroked her shoulders. "You remember that energy project I worked on, right?"

"Brescar, yes." One of Findlay's many research projects had involved the search for a suitable replacement for Essence in Ling Galaxy. As tall an order as that was, Findlay knew if he ever found a reliable substitute for Essence, that would've flipped the growing unrest about energy and controlling Essence delivery in Ling Galaxy on its head for sure. Unfortunately, Zakmar cut Findlay's hopes off, at least initially, when the Brescar project was ordered scrapped.

Findlay smiled. "I've found someone interested in working with me on Brescar besides Emperor Zakmar."

Charista's brow creased. "I thought that project was canceled."

Findlay shook his head. "More like delayed."

"Then who's working with you, another group in Omegana?"

"Not Omegan at all."

Charista froze. The idea of her father working with someone off world bothered her as much as the worry over if the news got around Omegan society and back to Zakmar himself.

"Dad, who?"

"Ander Pimm of the Railen."

Charista's eyes widened. The sworn enemy of the Omegans, the Railen were on their own quest for domination. But, while the Omegans wanted control of Ling Galaxy itself, the Railen aimed their sights on recapturing their lost home world of Grondia and Ling Galaxy by proxy. However, lofty goals were only dreams without the tools that made it happen.

His daughter's unease fairly obvious, Findlay said, "I know Zakmar doesn't take kindly to treason, which I'm sure includes dealing with the Railen. But I've thought about our situation and I feel like we're in a holding pattern here." Findlay's plans for their future included stability and freedom, neither of which seemed on the menu with being a solid Omegan citizen, as high up as he was in their chain.

Charista collected herself enough to speak again. "Is a deal with those ragtag bastard outcasts worth the risk?"

Findlay smiled. His daughter had very successfully reiterated the line fed to all Omegans from their collective education. "Don't forget, dear, the Railen were also outcast from the Nara. Omegans can't claim a genetic heritage with them, but our race served the Nara as guardians for centuries. As for the Railen, the race you learned about in school isn't the Railen race of now. Their resourcefulness made them a force to be reckoned with in short time. Remember, they have the key element a warrior needs: hunger. I believe they can get us where we want to be: a place of our own, hidden from Omegans where we can finally be free."

"Dad, I know you're no loyalist to Omegana and won't be heartbroken if we end up leaving here for good, but are you sure the Railen are our best bet?"

"I am, dear. I've met with Joanna, their scientific head. Our lives here are under a microscope. I'm followed and observed more each day. Zakmar's will to power is only checked by his chronic paranoia."

"What about Nic Sava and the UA? Maybe there's a chance for us there?" Charista asked.

"Sava and the UA are more politicians than anything. Sava wants to keep the status quo. He wouldn't ditch Essence; he's making too much money to do that. He's appeased Omegan aggression and Railen hostility for a while now. Besides, I'm hearing rumors Malone Stanton is interested in a deal with the Omegans, so no telling what changes come with that lunatic in the mix."

"What are you going to do then? There will be a war coming soon at this rate."

"I've no doubt. But wars mean opportunity for the clever. That's why I want to establish myself as an energy supplier, neutral, working for the highest bidder."

Charista marveled. While Findlay had typically been more of the scientific mind, Charista relished her father speaking more practically, even strategically, for a change. Findlay's world and work involved more formality, like regular meetings with Emperor Zakmar and other heads of state in Omegana. He had access to privileged info, but that came at a price of enhanced monitoring of his work by Omegan Security.

"But Dad, providing energy supply as an independent… you need protection for that."

"Of course, and that's where you come in. Once you complete training and get assigned into an Omegan military unit, you'll work yourself into a leadership role. Once we make our exit from Omegana, with your military might and my abilities, we'll build our own corner of Ling Galaxy that no one will ever be able to take away from us."

Charista's eyes widened. "Lead? Dad, that won't happen very fast. I'm just a graduation candidate right now. I'm barely known; definitely not a leader."

"The deal I'm negotiating with Ander Pimm will take at least a few months to come to fruition. Dear, are you forgetting how you brought in top marks in your training? Believe me, you're every bit the fighter your mother was. With the right effort and time, you'll be noticed, and soon."

Charista smiled at the thought. Her military future was still bittersweet, not having her mother alive to enjoy it too. Charista had faint childhood memories of her mother, Winola. The footage Charista watched of Winola addressing troops and leading Omegan detachments defending Nara on Essence runs were things she cherished very much.

Findlay said, "If the Railen come good on my first deal, that gets us money to start. We can look for soldiers for hire at first; and then, when we prove our worth, I bet more will join us."

Charista nodded, her brow furrowed. The mood overtook her sometimes, when she thought of her future and how she was cheated of sharing it with her mother.

Findlay, sensing her melancholy dip, grasped Charista's shoulder. As he'd done many times in the cycles since Winola's death, he felt himself putting out the good thoughts of what could be so the dread of what actually was stayed in the background. "It won't be easy, but I just know for us, no future of hope involves service to the Omegans."

"What about you, Dad?"

"I'm not much of a politician. My best work is done in research and science. It's better I worry about the logistical side of our plan. You, on the other hand, have your mother's charisma. It's best we fight this problem from two ends. I'll make my arrangements with Ander Pimm, and you propel yourself further into the ranks militarily."

"I'm one of dozens graduating, Dad. Everyone wants the choice details."

"Do your work. Make contacts. Volunteer for the tough assignments. You'll get there faster; I just know it. The

Omegans will be moving into more systems soon, and they'll need able bodied field leaders like you."

"Somehow, I thought your news was going to be a cure for Veculus." Charista sighed. "My friend, Phoebe, has it now."

'It' was sufficient enough a pronoun for any citizen in Ling Galaxy to understand it meant Veculus. The horrible virus had mysteriously circulated the Galaxy for many cycles and infected a large number of citizens from various races. Only a few, like the Nara and the Railen, showed immunity from it to that point. This fed wide speculation that Veculus was a biological weapon sent into Ling Galaxy by the Nara in an attempt at maintaining control over their operations.

The Omegana system had joined the ranks of worlds infected with Veculus long ago, and Gajanan, the capital city where Findlay and Charista lived, was no exception.

Findlay clutched Charista's shoulder. "Phoebe, huh?"

"She's been placed with the quarantine."

Findlay shuddered. The quarantine was the last ditched effort in a fight with no reasonable option. Large portions of the Omegan population infected with Veculus were brought off Omegana to a distant moon, where they spent all their time in an isolated community made of sectioned areas. The mere description of it sounded more like a prison than a medical healing facility. To many, the thought of being sent there was one worse than death, especially given the low number of patients who were ever known to have returned alive from the Omegan quarantine colony.

Findlay hoped Charista hadn't noticed the fear he felt as it simmered in his gut. "How long has Phoebe known?"

"A few days. When the fever didn't break for a week, she had herself checked, and they confirmed it."

"I'm sorry, dear. I know the latest attempted vaccine failed to stop it." Findlay quickly got to his feet.

Charista was soon at her father's side; it was her turn to be comforter. "I know, Dad, I know." She wrapped her arm around Findlay's drooped shoulders. They both knew the next part of the story; it went unsaid as they both paused in their memories. Besides a few video clips, Charista only had Findlay's stories about her mother to cling to, one of them being her death from Veculus.

Findlay felt buoyed by his daughter's love as, together with Charista, they relished his lost wife and her lost mother. "She was a good woman, tried and true, one of the best Omegana ever produced."

"The best." Charista echoed his words through a whimper before her tear-filled eyes locked with Findlay's. Many of Charista's memories of her mother were through the stories of Findlay, as Charista was a young child when Winola died.

"She gave her all for Omegana, and there isn't even a statue or a plaque for her. How could they just forget her like that?"

Findlay said nothing at first, but only slipped his arm around his daughter. "Zakmar likes to paint his own history, and whatever doesn't make him out to be the savior of all Omegans gets pushed aside. Don't think for a moment I've forgotten what happened to your mother. Not for one instant. Every day I get up, go to my work, meet my marks, satisfy quotas, and keep in the back of my head that one thing above all: to honor her. She wasn't worth the time to Omegana, but she will be honored by us. We will both do that, in our time."

Charista nodded and slunk downward into a chair in thought. She was almost at the end of the adolescent phase of her

Omegan development, and with it came a marked degree of impatience. She activated a holo screen as a distraction. The display leaped in front of her in a midair projection that displayed a collection of games available.

Findlay lay his hands on Charista's shoulders, kneading them softly. She smiled at the gesture of affection. Findlay had struggled to fill the gap left by Winola, and he did as much as he could, sometimes to Charista's amusement. But she couldn't have denied feeling the love her father showed her through all the cycles without her mother.

"It's all going to work out." Findlay smiled. "Ander's willing to set up a plant to distribute the Brescar once he can secure proper replication capabilities. And feeding him tidbits on what the Omegans are up to has given us a pretty good entry point with them."

"Are you sure the Omegans won't get wind of what you've been doing? It's pretty dangerous, Dad."

"Sometimes danger is a necessary risk, my dear." Findlay shrugged.

"So, why can't you replicate here?"

"Because, Zakmar commandeered my replication facilities. They're only interested in making weapons and crafts for their exploits. Brescar is less than an afterthought. They don't like the instability."

"Instability?"

"I've seen it lance holes through the time spectrum, even space spectrum. I've been interested in exploring those, but not while Zakmar's waving the war banner. I've been put on notice for assistance in weapons development, and if I'm going to keep up this charade with the Omegans and still get my part of the bargain with the Railen, I must act as though I'm playing along, at least for now."

Findlay took a calming breath before he continued. "Of all the things I've done, setting up your future is my top goal. Your mother and I..." Emotion finished Findlay's thought as he clutched his midsection in a sob. Charista hugged her father, and sadness for his and her situation flooded her, along with a hatred for the indifference their government showed at their situation.

"You're taking Brescar for this plan; don't you think they'll notice enough of it missing to be a problem for us?"

"No, I've got a reserve quantity for development. Anyway, if you listen to the likes of Chun, he's only interested in conquest. Fuel is a minor concern, as much as Essence in Ling Galaxy is in dispute. My position with the Science Wing of Omegana doesn't carry enough weight. There's too much for them to focus on in Ling Galaxy without worrying about my developments. They'll gladly fuel their ships up, but the interest and gratitude stop there. My friend, Joanna, has seen to it to make this deal possible, and I think it's the best we've got so far."

Charista shrugged. The loss of her mother was too great for her to shake off, and she resented Findlay at times because he seemed too little emotionally ravaged externally for Charista's liking. But she knew, in time, her turn for making plans would come. Whether it be with the help of the Railen or by her own doing, vengeance stayed in Charista's sight, even if it was still out of reach.

"For now, my dear, we've got to keep going. Every day, think of Winola, what she'd want for us, and make it happen." Findlay saw both sides of the Omegan machine and the Railen as pawns in his own game. His only fear was in discovery before his position became powerful enough.

## Chapter 2

THE FOLLOWING DAY, FINDLAY MET WITH the other heads of Omegana for their regular session with Emperor Zakmar. Over the past thirty cycles since their separation from Nara service, the Omegan race grew at a very healthy pace. Their abilities and physical strength at least extended their survival in Ling Galaxy, a place where want was more known than satisfaction.

The Omegan goals were uncomplicated. Their history was filled with subservience to the Nara. From early times, the Omegans served as protective force for the Nara, once the Nara deemed their own security an overreach of their mission. The Omegans provided protection to the Nara on their missions of Essence delivery in Ling Galaxy.

Omegan service to the Nara had lasted for centuries, and while it wasn't without trouble from bands of marauders and smugglers trying to grab some of the precious element to Ling

Galaxy, the Omegans prided themselves on a regular run of service until the Nara released them.

Like other races in Ling Galaxy, the Omegans dealt with their own trials and sufferings. Illness hit a large portion of their population and, while potential medications existed, the width of Ling Galaxy and the number affected made treatments for all beyond reasonable. The Omegans counted their dead, and when the numbers grew too large for them to tolerate, they took action.

Zakmar led the charge for change. Staging a coup, he overthrew the existing Omegan ruler and established a firm presence for the Omegans. No longer would they be known as former hand servants of the Nara, following and obeying their directions. The Omegans' new purpose was of conquest, of order, and of domination in Ling Galaxy.

Never one for modesty, Zakmar reclined against his opulent chair and gazed on the faces of his military and scientific heads. "We've come a long way. Omegans no longer stoop in service to others, but have stood in declaration of our superiority. We've spread our empire to other systems in Ling Galaxy, and every day our foothold increases. But our path forward isn't always clear. We've got obstacles, and there are those who want more than anything to see us fail. I want to know what happened at the Bertold system."

The room went deathly silent. Part of the Omegan conquest involved setting up encampments on strategic systems in Ling Galaxy for coordinated operations. The mission of the Omegans was clear: capture, raid as many systems for supplies as possible, render any opposition encountered inert. The UA forces fought the Omegans to a point, but the stretch of the UA in Ling Galaxy left many of their units less able to hold off the

Omegan onslaught. Nic Sava with the UA opted for a policy of sanctions against the Omegans, a punishment Zakmar regarded as a mere taunt. While the Omegans hadn't yet tipped the balance of systems in Ling Galaxy to their favor, Zakmar's primary goal was making that happen as soon as possible.

The Omegan pack hunting method had proved successful; at the very least it gave them a handy supply of reinforcements for those who ran into trouble they weren't able to handle on their own.

However, one of these operations was disrupted by the Railen attack on the Bertold system. What further concerned Zakmar was the utter secrecy of the operation. Not even the average Omegan citizen knew about military operations like the one on Bertold, at least not information specific enough for an ambush like this required, so the betrayer among them was part of a select group.

Findlay swallowed hard. While he wasn't on the immediate hook for answering his leader, he knew full well his part in the Railen attack. He tensed his midsection and attempted his best at invisibility. He'd felt himself in this position more and more since his deal with the Railen had begun, and he leaned on a mantra when his fears reached a point he was afraid might have caused him to break down and reveal himself. He sucked in slow breaths and repeated to himself: *I am safe, I am hidden, I am fine.*

Findlay's meditation was broken up when Yul Mailey managed to clear his throat. At once, the attention of the room shot to him.

"Colonel Mailey, you have something to share with us?" Zakmar completed his sentence with a deep-set scowl.

Yul nodded and, after a slight stammering, began, "My Lord, we were fortified in our defenses; we'd begun deployment of our heavy weaponry when we were caught by surprise. I'm afraid our forces were unable to respond quick enough, and the encampment was lost."

Zakmar steepled his fingers and eyed Yul. Zakmar found it best, when he received a report on a failed operation, that he first allowed the responsible party enough time for their brief on all information pertinent to what went wrong. "I see. So, you claim your defenses were set and strong. So then, how is it that you were overrun, engaged, and defeated by a group like the Railen?"

Yul's brow creased, and his breaths quickened. Zakmar thrust a palm in Yul's direction. "Do we all know the Railen? I'm assuming we're aware of them. As strong as the Omegans are, surely we're aware of any of the races who pose a mild threat to us."

"A race of renegades," Commander Patrach offered, giving his junior officer a brief rest from the hot seat. "Bastard children of the Nara, expelled for crimes against Nara society, genetically altered and thrown into Ling Galaxy to forage and find an existence permanently cut off from their birth home."

"Renegades," repeated Zakmar as he stood, his hands flattened against the table and his head facing downward. "Given a meager existence from the UA, barely enough means for even the simplest space travel. How then did they even get word of our location and manage this attack?"

"They're destitute, but hardly helpless," offered Patrach. "Some of the better minds from Nara were in that group. The lost yet resourceful can find their way with the right kind of effort. We cannot discount their inventive spirit. Our own scouts have come across the Railen, organized off world into several sub fleets."

Zakmar arched a brow. "Go on?"

"Their ships are mismatched, but their desire and skill are indisputable. We're also talking about some of the best Nara military produced, as we may remember, the very race that once trained ours. While I won't speak for their worth against Omegan muscle, they aren't the cowering wretches we'd like to believe. We should never count them out, with all due respect, my Lord."

"Fair enough," Zakmar growled. "But aggression against our own never goes unchecked under my rule. The Railen grow in power, this I accept for now. That doesn't mean I choose to flat out ignore it. They've struck at us; so we now revisit that transgression with every bit of vengeance I know lies at the heart of every Omegan. It's that desire for retribution that led me to assume control; it's that hunger for power that made me want to lead this crusade."

Zakmar aimed his eyes back to Yul for a moment. "Omegans are destined to rule Ling Galaxy. One day it will be reality, not just words. That said, we will not achieve rule if we cannot hold our own against lesser races. Are you comprehending me, Colonel Yul?"

Yul nodded quickly; his eyes cast downward.

Zakmar stood and walked around the room. Findlay felt beads of sweat itching their way down his scalp and forehead. He thought back to the times of Zakmar's inspections of the Science Wing. The reviews of even the scientific developments by Zakmar were extremely detailed, which always had Findlay worried he'd taken care of everything.

Zakmar kept a very hands-on approach throughout his rule. Findlay figured it was because of the nature of how Zakmar assumed power. A ruler crowned out of deceit lived with the possibility of a coup done in kind back to him.

Findlay felt his heart seize when Zakmar passed directly behind him. Like his fellow attendees, Findlay searched the words and even the tone of Zakmar. These meetings were known for being displays of discipline for any who stepped out of line in their emperor's eyes.

"Our efforts will continue. We keep our Horde deployed, groups in close proximity to each other. Our operations to overtake Ling Galaxy continue. Tell your troops to a soldier to do all that is necessary: infiltrate, take, destroy, capture the able bodied for our slave work. The phony benefactors of the UA and the smug Nara will one day kneel before Omegan might, of this I'm sure. The Railen think they deserve some recompense for their slight. While I've no love for the Nara, the Railen will learn the price of crossing the Omegans."

Zakmar stopped his circular procession once he got behind Yul's chair. With one hand on the seatback, Zakmar pawed the handle of his ceremonial Omegan blade. It was the customary adornment for Omegan rulers. As the story went, the weapon's steel had etched markings of early Omegans and tarnishes from bloodstains added by Zakmar when he did in his predecessor at the height of his coup.

Zakmar glanced across the table to Findlay for a moment before he looked to Commander Chun. "Commander Chun, take a company of Omegan ships and ground troops to the Railen settlement. Teach them a lesson. Let them know Omegan blood spilled will be revisited tenfold."

Chun grinned hungrily. "It will be a pleasure, my Lord. We'll eliminate them from existence."

"No," Zakmar corrected his liege. "Kill many, but leave some intact. I want Ander Pimm and his kind to see the result of their foolish move."

As Chun nodded, Zakmar pulled the blade from its sheath, and in one fluid movement, jut the blade through the back of Yul's chair, until the tip of the blade burst through Yul's chest. Yul responded with a loud yell as he slumped forward, his body drenched with a gushing pool of greyish blood on the table. The others seated nearby gasped. Those closest to Yul's fresh corpse recoiled from the spray. Findlay felt a tremor through his core as he attempted to swallow the lump that remained in his throat.

"Let this be an object lesson for any who doubt my orders in the future," Zakmar muttered blankly before he sheathed his blade and exited the room.

## Chapter 3

AFTER THE MEETING WITH ZAKMAR and the other Omegan heads, Findlay returned to his private communications chamber where he contacted Joanna. Unlike when he spoke with Ander Pimm, where the feeling was filled with worry and doubt, with Joanna there was an ease, a calmness. Joanna was a kindred spirit, an intellectual type like Findlay, and she was under appreciated in her past position with the Nara. She knew what it meant to be important to someone.

Joanna had also been a bright spot in the mostly worried hours of Findlay's life. She even showed concern for how Findlay was handling Winola's absence. Findlay was still amazed how they initially ran into each other.

Findlay's designation as head of the Omegan Science Wing gave him flexibility similar to the Omegan military. Trips off

Omegana were common for Findlay, and his craft was designed to indicate scientific research far more than military aggression. As a result, he was typically ignored by the marauders and other warlike types in the Galaxy.

Findlay made a lot of excursions in his search for the elements of Brescar. Initially working on a suitable alternative to Essence, he began to look for more exotic matter and found several locations of it in Ling Galaxy. His mining spots were typically on remote moons and far less traveled places, making his work rather isolated and lonely. He comforted himself with his end goal: the substance that all races in Ling Galaxy, even Omegans, would be unable to function without. This alternative to Essence would then establish Omegana as the ultimate power.

Findlay had been off on a scouting mission, mining for precious elements in his work on Brescar, when he happened upon a Railen expedition as well. His Omegan background had him on guard at first, as the Railen were also. It was Joanna, leader of the Railen expedition, who eased his mind. Something about her relaxed him. Findlay thought perhaps it was a look in Joanna's eyes that he'd seen in Winola's that gave him an island of warmth in his sea of cold scientific search.

He had managed secret contacts with Joanna since that day, and it was she who gave Findlay an in to the Railen Network and meeting Ander Pimm.

Findlay felt an odd kinship with Joanna on many levels. Their respective scientific distinctions from their diametrically opposed races gave them more than enough for endless conversation, but they both shared a bond over their placement in the realm of the unappreciated.

Findlay even found a place of bonding with Joanna on the subject of his wife's demise. The more he spoke with Joanna, the more comfortable he felt with her, but it never eased his worries about what the contact with her meant to his own government and the punishment he faced if caught.

"How are you holding up?" Joanna asked.

Findlay chuckled for a moment. "Hardly anyone asks me that. I'm surviving. I keep my eyes on the end goal and tell myself everything I'm doing will get Charista and me there. I just have to believe in the deals I made."

"And how is lovely Charista?" Joanna asked.

"Fine. Fit. About to graduate and take on the Galaxy. She's her mother's daughter, no doubt."

Joanna studied her friend for a while before she continued. "Have you told her?"

"About my deal with the Railen? Of course. She deserves to know."

"No." Joanna's eyes bled compassion for her friend. "You know what I mean."

Findlay froze. Of course, he knew. Joanna's reminder wasn't necessary. She only brought it up out of her growing concern for Findlay, someone whose contact had over time gone the way from amiable colleague to emotional partner.

"I haven't, I can't tell her that, I—"

"It wasn't your fault, Findlay." Joanna clutched the screen. Findlay smiled weakly at the gesture. It had happened naturally between them. Their initial professional demeanor gave way to a tension-filled relationship of subterfuge, where she offered something Findlay rarely had except with Charista: a confidant unjudging and concerned for his welfare.

Joanna's eyes pleaded with him. "Zakmar made you inject Winola with a Veculus culture under threat of killing Charista if you didn't."

Findlay winced from Joanna's words; he sank back into his chair as a wave of grief cascaded over him. "Every day since I've had to live with that. Every moment I wake up and know she's not with us and I'm the reason why. Each time I see her eyes in my daughter's—how can I tell her I'm the one who did that to Winola?"

Joanna's mouth formed a line. "Listen to me, dear. You're a scientific genius. Your life's desire is for discovery and for making the world around you better. Is there glory in that? Sure, sometimes. Regardless, you want to rest your head knowing you made a difference. Winola wanted the same thing, to make a difference for her people, the nation she loved. But she saw her leader going out of control, and she did what anyone who loved their nation would've... she tried to stop him."

Findlay desperately wanted to believe the things Joanna told him, about his place and how his work wasn't to blame, but he wasn't ready to believe it yet.

Joanna continued, "You're given us a chance to expand our reach, and that won't go unrewarded, I can assure you. I've got the ear of Ander Pimm, consider me a direct line to him."

Findlay nodded.

Joanna continued, "With our improved ability, our presence in Ling Galaxy is continuing. All we need from you is more information on the movements of Omegans, like the Bertold System maneuver. We will work out of their sight as much as possible, confronting them with force only when necessary. We've already located a place for you and Charista. It's secure and, with the Replication technology we plan to acquire on the Zormad system, we will soon be in a very desirable position."

"Sounds good to me. And our arrangement stays in effect?" Findlay swallowed hard. While his plans of being a major energy supplier were largely driven by his scientific urges, he knew in the end, a solid funding source and the ability to hire enough of a garrison for his safety was the key ingredient he needed. The financial aspect of his agreement with the Railen was the last bit of his insurance policy over his goals.

Joanna paused for a moment then replied, "Our deal is intact, as much as I can say."

Findlay tensed. Any uncertainty tested him. "Joanna, I have to know we're solid. I've given you fuel in good faith; don't forget I can make that unavailable very quickly."

Joanna's brow arched. "You have to understand, Ander gets more driven daily. He gives me new directives all the time. The best I can tell you for now is all is as it was. Please believe me."

Findlay sighed. "I guess that'll do for now. Have you thought about my other offer?"

Joanna demurred slightly. "Joining you?"

Findlay nodded.

Joanna glanced downward, then back. "I do think about it. A lot has to happen first before I can do more than think about it. Please keep the faith, dear. We'll be in touch."

Findlay rubbed the sides of his head in thought. "We're in a place, aren't we?"

"Absolutely. Remember when it was just about the science?"

Findlay ran a finger down Joanna's jawline on-screen. Her smile deepened. Findlay then recited the mantra they'd made together, as a way of focusing their anxieties about the dangers ahead. Joanna joined in as he spoke, "Our futures aren't set, but with faith will become reality."

Findlay kissed his palm and touched the screen. "Until later, my love."

"Bye for now." Joanna nodded.

Regardless of what became of Findlay's plans with Joanna, the Railen, and his Omegan subterfuge, he knew Charista deserved the truth. He hated how he'd kept it in for so long, but the practice became just another one of his many running deceptions.

## Chapter 4

FINDLAY PLAYED BACK THE MEMORY in his mind often. While the pains he felt over how he lost Winola were strong, he resigned himself to the pangs being something he deserved. In Findlay's mind, no one who did what he'd done deserved any measure of peace.

Since Zakmar had assumed rule of Omegana after he dispatched Anton, the former Emperor, he'd devoted his energies and those of Omegana to canvasing Ling Galaxy and establishing Omegana as a proper ruling entity. This brought them in contact with the Universal Alliance on more than one occasion, with the associated skirmishes and, sometimes, full out battles as a result.

Among the ranks, leading troops as a proper Omegana general, was Winola Mantisword. She carried out her duties according to her oath. But even the most devoted soldier suffered the occasional bouts of second guessing, in particular when the homeland population of Omegana began suffering with more cases of Veculus.

After many discussions with Findlay and seeing firsthand Zakmar's devotion only to conquering worlds without caring for his own, Winola made her attempt at assassinating Zakmar. Unfortunately, the support Winola drummed up among fellow military wasn't nearly enough, and she was caught before her plans were ever carried out.

Zakmar insisted on addressing her personally, and after an in-depth session with Winola and Findlay to determine exactly the depth of the insurrection, Zakmar knew he needed a public display and a statement. The Emperor needed his people to know that even a high ranking General of Omegana wasn't immune from the most severe punishment for treason.

Zakmar had Findlay escorted to his private chambers, where Findlay stood, his innards knotted up with fear he'd never felt before.

"I can't have officers doing things behind my back like Winola was," Zakmar began. He paced about the room, his eyes narrowed in deep thought, while Findlay was frozen in place.

"I've seen the reports that you weren't involved in this coup. However, being the spouse of the offender doesn't exactly get you off without a mark."

Findlay swallowed hard. "I understand."

"I give you a choice, one you can discuss with Winola. We need an example of how this betrayal won't be tolerated at all. The choice you have is Winola's life... or yours."

Findlay's legs buckled. A million regrets shot through him... *why did Winola even try what she did? If she'd gotten more*

*support, could it have worked? I can't lose her! No, take me,*
*please!*

Zakmar, smiled slightly at the sight of Findlay in a horrible
game of bargaining with himself. He decided to sweeten the pot
even more.

"Director Mantisword, I'd accept the life of your daughter
instead."

#

Findlay took a break from his memories, worries, and plans.
He walked into the storehouse area of his facility, where lay his
prized creation, Brescar. Other than his dear departed wife and
devoted daughter, nothing roused more pride in him.

The greenish liquid swirled around in the large containers that
held it. Findlay stared at his creation through the windows of
the holding bins and wondered just where Brescar was going to
take him. He'd lost his faith in his government, but in his family
and his creation, he placed the fate of himself without question.

While Essence was the ultimate jewel in Findlay's mind,
many relied on the standard fuel cells in Ling Galaxy as a
dependable source of energy. The challenge with standard fuel
cells usually lay with supply, however; while the UA had the
majority of fuel cells, they weren't altogether safely hidden.
And the enterprising and daring, like the Omegans, found
themselves with a regular supply as a reward for a little elbow
grease and an occasional theft. Findlay knew that, besides the
Omegans, the Railen would be in a race for that as well; and the
Railen had a slightly more strategic attitude about their search,
which made them much more attractive to Findlay when it came
time for making a deal.

Findlay's efforts at creating Brescar weren't successful for
very long, and it was only through the grace of Zakmar's

allowances that he was allowed to continue. The primary demand of Omegana on Findlay lay in the development of armaments and weaponry, which he complied with the most Machiavellian of attitudes.

Findlay fed Zakmar scraps of his brilliance in Findlay's hope that he would one day be able to satisfy his own appetite for rewards in the future.

For a brief moment, Findlay thought he'd actually done it and found his way into Omegan legend in the process. Time and the stubborn attitude he'd prided himself on since his youth eventually rewarded him. Brescar proved a viable fuel source, letting the Omegan fleet venture even further than the standard fuel elements in Ling Galaxy had allowed. However, Brescar's birth was not without complications, and instabilities in the fuel source showed up before long.

The problems with Brescar began, when several ships and groups of Omegans vanished from Ling Galaxy without a trace. The best calculations run by Findlay's team indicated the volatility of Brescar sent their ships through a hole in spacetime. After that, Zakmar ordered Brescar to be removed from ship fuel sources, returning to the standard fuel cell system used throughout Ling Galaxy. The rationale by Zakmar was that their eventual conquest of Ling Galaxy would bring with it all the fuel they needed, making Brescar, in the eyes of Zakmar and those who valued his word, ancillary at best.

Per Zakmar, Findlay's development was quickly buried in the Omegan arsenal. Outwardly, Findlay knew better than to flash indignation at his leader's contempt of Findlay's prized creation. Charista knew how her father felt about the shunning, even though Findlay never spoke much about it. Findlay had been denied the glory of his single most important contribution to Ling Galaxy at large. It was only then he seriously entertained the notion that his ultimate goals would've only been reached with the help of those from outside his own race. His chance encounter with Joanna further amplified his thoughts on this and it soon determined his chosen path.

It wasn't until Findlay's contact with Joanna Yamak that Findlay saw a possible use for his prized creation after all, and Brescar went from the bottom of the Omegan trash heap, aka research archives, to the forefront of the future for Findlay and his family.

Even though Brescar was abandoned, there remained, on hand, a healthy enough supply, enough for collateral for Findlay's plan. The Railen were an eager bidder, needing a quick source of energy for their own aims, and Findlay realized how much his ultimate creation was worth, once and for all.

Findlay stood on an observation platform and watched his creation. Zakmar decided the remnants of Brescar would be used only as an alternative to the standard fuel cells in Ling Galaxy. The instability was too big a concern, and Zakmar wasn't interested in any more missteps.

Findlay rested his head on his clasped hands on the observation platform railing as he admired his creation. "You're my life's work. You'll make me the greatest inventor in the history of Ling Galaxy. Ander Pimm thinks he can work me and take what he wants, but he'll see. One day, they'll all see. I'll be the one they all come to, once they see the true capabilities of Brescar."

Findlay beamed in the knowledge as his plans synthesized like the most complex of scientific theories. However, the certainty of things coming together as much as they appeared to worried him that much more.

*Zakmar has the Galaxy in his grasp, but he's short sighted. He's worried about conquest and power and not as much about what comes afterward. People vanquished but still hungry are dangerous. Want leads to discord and, if unchecked, grows into rebellion. He won't keep every discontented race in Ling Galaxy under his boot. Before long, he'll have other upstarts trying to topple what he's built for himself.*

Findlay noticed a nearby stack of loading crates and felt his pulse quicken. These were another in the line of his bargain with the Railen. These shipments were his ticket, for him and Charista, the paper on which he was signing the deal for their future. He'd worried about the Railen, but all things considered, he felt not much better about what he had with the Omegans. At least the Railen had shown interest in his plans and what their end result could be.

## Chapter 5

TO FINDLAY, COMMANDER PATRACH was a distant second behind Emperor Zakmar in getting Findlay in his most tense and defensive state. When Findlay was summoned to Omegan Military Command by Patrach himself, his mind became a muddle of thoughts. He reviewed his mantra in his mind, repeated it as much as he could when the fears over what lay ahead for him weren't too great for him to focus.

While Findlay had known Patrach from their youth, the two were never close. Omegans were divided from early cycles once their best abilities were determined, and their socialization and training were held in a social quarantine apart from those with different designations. The soldiers only grew and were nurtured in an environment that fostered the best in warrior skills and training. The scientifically minded were fostered in a realm where their intellectual grasp knew no boundaries, nor were they forced to wait for the lesser minded to grasp their complex diet of information.

Findlay was greeted by two sentries at the entrance of Omegan Military Command. The large imposing figures stood a width apart. Each were covered with Omegan battle armor and shouldered a heavy pulse rifle. The Omegan military industrial complex was, no doubt, the dominant force in Omegan culture; and the fact their own command center had this level of security was a statement, for sure.

Once Findlay awkwardly explained his summons, the two soldiers wordlessly escorted him through the complex. One guard walked before Findlay, the other behind. After several minutes of this, Findlay found himself in the communications center, where he faced Commander Patrach.

"It's been a while, hasn't it?" Patrach's face showed the slightest hint of warmth.

"A while, general?"

"Since our cycles of training." Patrach's eyes narrowed.

Findlay felt a knot in his throat as he nodded. "Of course, yes. I didn't know if you'd remember me."

"How could I not? You were top of your class in the sciences. I think most Omegans in our class remember that. It's not as exciting as the military track, granted, but you have to admire anyone who achieves the best in their chosen field."

Findlay had almost felt like he could relax when Patrach's gaze got cold. "Director Mantisword, I'm troubled."

Commander Patrach's statement was enough to get Findlay's pulse running again. He lived on a jagged edge, in the knowledge that at any moment, any misstep he may have made could've led the Omegans back to him, including the discovery that the slipup at the encampment on Bertold was his fault, not

Yul's. Now another death was added to the fallout of Findlay's gambit.

"I see. What's the matter?" Findlay asked.

Patrach motioned Findlay to a bank of screens, operated by an Omegan soldier. Patrach motioned to a screen to the top. "As you know, we regularly monitor activity in Ling Galaxy, broadcasts on Network and such. But we also keep an eye on our own transmissions, and I've been seeing some activity from your scientific wing that is a little out of the ordinary."

*Out of the ordinary?* Findlay thought. His agitated mind tried working out all possibilities for what Patrach had seen, but before too long, Joanna came up foremost in his mind.

*That was my secure channel. I thought they'd stopped monitoring me like they did around Winola's sentencing.*

The glum realization settled in: If Findlay had done anything at all, even something totally different, to raise suspicion, the door would've been opened to all of his activities. He feared that his privacy was already a casualty in his cause before he even realized it.

Findlay's body stiffened. He quickly reminded himself that his ruse, his performance, wasn't one that involved an intermission. "I see. I know we've been running some research on weapon development; maybe some of those projects reached outward into Network and beyond?"

Patrach eyed Findlay for several moments, waiting for Findlay's resolve, studying for any cracks that could be exploited to see the inner truth behind the fractures. Findlay did his best at steeling himself, but inwardly he shrank like a witness under brutal cross examination. Outwardly, Findlay kept his moderate cool, enough that Patrach wondered if his tension was the average reaction of the non-military warrior facing a direct examination from one of Omegana's most notorious fighters.

Findlay shifted on his feet. He'd watched Winola over their time together; she was a practiced warrior and had kept her cool in situations way worse than Findlay faced. Findlay was thankful Charista took after her mother in that respect. For Findlay, the endless pursuit of development and discovery left little time for things like strategic maneuvering, and he only got somewhere strategic with his special development of Brescar.

Patrach studied the bank of communications in silence for a few moments. "Director Mantisword, have you made any more developments on Brescar?" His eyes quickly returned to Findlay's.

"Of course not."

"I'm very glad to hear that, and I do hope it's the truth. I will remind you, Emperor Zakmar is grateful for your contributions, but he insists all your efforts are directed to our military enterprises for the foreseeable future. I trust your current station and the welfare of your daughter is enough for your compliance?"

"Of course, it is." Findlay had almost gotten used to saying the lies. Thinking about protecting Charista in the process helped him.

"Director Mantisword, we'll be monitoring your transmissions closely as a precaution. You say you're involved in research, and I will hold you to that, but know that we are watching you. Anything further that raises suspicion will be brought to the attention of Emperor Zakmar and will be treated with the utmost concern. I advise you to remember Colonel Yul and his current state."

Findlay's lips drew in tight, and he managed a quick sigh as he steadied himself as best as possible. "Message received. Hail Omegana."

Once he was returned to the entrance, Findlay hurried back to his dwelling. The net had been cast, and time for him was running short. He hoped the plans he'd set in mind were more than just hopes. A very uneasy tightness swept over him at the realization the time for giving his beloved daughter the truth about his role in her mother's death was upon him. Since his move could've meant the end of him, he knew that more than anything he owed Charista the truth.

## Chapter 6

"WE'RE RUNNING OUT OF TIME."

Findlay writhed his hands together as his train of thought once again went on a wild ride. All his plans, his hopes, the future he had in mind for him and Charista hung in the balance as Commander Patrach closed in on him quickly.

When he looked back at Charista, his body shook. "They've stepped up their monitoring on me, Charista, and now with the attack on Zakmar's fleet, it's getting harder to keep my cover. It's possible I've already been made, in fact."

Findlay clasped his arms and sat down, rocking back and forth in tension. Charista sat next to her father. "What do you think they know?"

"Patrach has monitored me; I don't think they know anything, but then again, they'd want me to think they don't know so they can find out as much as they can find out about me."

"There has to be something we can do."

"I've considered everything. The Railen are so far holding true on their agreement, but the moment it comes out about my betrayal, I'll be executed rather brutally, most likely on a feed to all Omegan citizens as an example. There's no tolerance for this kind of slight." Findlay buried his face in his hands as he sunk in to the chair.

Charista, moved at the sight of her father's anguish, snaked her arm around him. She felt as helpless as she'd ever been and rested her face against his trembling frame. "I hate them. Their promises are all empty. They want conquest, but they don't care about their own who suffer. Zakmar is so blinded by his quest for power that he neglects his best and brightest no matter what they do for him."

Findlay felt safe in the embrace of his daughter, enough that his worries flooded out of him. His voice trembled when he spoke again. "I refuse to let something happen to you. If they find out about me, they'll instantly assume you were involved, and you'll be likely imprisoned at the very best or killed along with me as a further example. Zakmar has no issue with enforcing the maximum penalty so everyone knows exactly what it means to cross him."

Findlay knew the moment was upon him. He ran from much, but the truth had gained too much ground on him. He realized if his end was near, he owed it to Charista to set the record straight about her mother. Charista eyed him with concern that mirrored Findlay's feverish expression.

"What?" Charista asked.

"I have to tell you something about your mother."

Charista blinked. "Uh huh?"

"I've told you about her, all these stories about how wonderful she was, because I wanted you to know them, to know her, the kind of Omegan she was. And that is all true, but I wasn't truthful about how she died."

Charista's mouth hung agape. She leaned backward in her seat. "What are you talking about?"

"We saw where Zakmar was going. His violent coup, the people he slaughtered, and we felt that he'd led us closer to destruction than conquering. Your mother and I agreed that Zakmar was stretching Omegan numbers too thin while our people at home were neglected. Still, Zakmar attacked UA installations while Omegana floundered. So, your mother struck back. She was out to kill Zakmar himself at the time when she was double crossed."

Charista asked, "Did Zakmar kill her?"

"Not exactly." Findlay took a shaky breath. "She was returned and questioned. It wasn't much of a fair hearing; they had enough evidence stacked up against her. She was branded a traitor, and Zakmar demanded a severe punishment for her so everyone knew what happened to those who challenged him."

"I studied torture in the Omegan Academy, the methods used to extract information or just to cause pain when that's the goal," Charista said. "What did they do, injections?"

The word shot through Findlay like a knife. Charista felt her insides go cold as she searched the eyes of her father. Findlay's answer to Charista wasn't spoken, but she'd already heard it loud and clear through Findlay's agonized gaze.

"Y-you? You killed her?"

"They forced me to. If I didn't do it, it would've been someone else. Dear, you must understand how much it has ripped me apart ever since."

Charista looked away. She felt her pulse as it throbbed in her throat. "What did you give her?"

"Charista, it doesn't—"

"What did you give her?" Charista's eyes bored into Findlay's.

"Veculus."

Charista narrowed her eyes at Findlay.

Findlay shrugged. "We had a culture of it, since we'd been working on vaccines. Zakmar wanted an example to show that not even his greatest general was immune from punishment for crossing him."

Findlay looked off, terrified at seeing his daughter's face again. He felt her hand slowly slip from his and saw Charista stand over him.

Her voice shuddered when she spoke again. "You killed my mother? How could you have let that happen? What were you thinking? Aren't you supposed to be the greatest scientific mind in Omegana?"

Charista headed for the door.

"Charista, there's more; you have to listen!"

But Charista had heard enough. She left the room and their dwelling, and sank into a sea of despair.

## Chapter 7

C HARISTA RAN OUTSIDE, CRYING BITTERLY. The cool evening air would've been pleasant, if it wasn't for the dreadful truth she was given. A thousand emotions battled for control over Charista. The torment soon gave way to a burst of energy, and Charista Mantisword took off in a full running sprint to nowhere in particular.

After a while, she felt burning in her limbs, strengthened through military training, but pushed to their limits through her sadness and rage over her father's confession. Still, she edged herself further.

She ran past Omegan buildings and the government complex in the city of Gajanan. She held in her mind her mother's face, and wondered: *How could Dad do that to me?* She was lost in a sea of emotions and questions with no hope for flotation.

Finally, her lungs had enough and she fell to the ground. Between her sobs, she punched the ground repeatedly. "Why?

Why did you do this?" she cried out to no one. A question she knew in her every fiber was unanswerable for the rest of her days.

Findlay saw and heard nothing of his daughter for a week. Not even a glimpse of her around their home the day of graduation; she remained invisible, throwing herself into physical training at the Omegan Military facility. For Charista, it was the best possible solution until she figured out what her next move was.

The Omegan Military facility included housing for troops and trainees, and Charista was allowed access as a recent graduate. It was the only place she felt close to her mother or what her mother had been. She gladly took one of the bunks reserved for the training classes as the next round weren't set to start for another month.

She strained her mind for memories of her mother and knew there was nothing she could've come up with. But while her mother wasn't a memory she could dredge, Charista realized she had access to someone besides Findlay who may have known more about what happened.

Charista activated the comm. She'd seen Findlay's settings when he reached out to Joanna. As much as it drew unwanted attention on her, she needed to know all she could about what happened and just what had possessed Findlay.

Charista's transmission wasn't answered on the first several tries. She soon realized Joanna was probably careful and not accepted any contact from a pure Omegan signal.

Time to improvise, she thought. She didn't have access to Findlay's private signal, but she had something that was worth a chance.

Charista scrawled the message that she'd heard Findlay say to Joanna on their conversations when Charista was conveniently eavesdropping while denying she'd heard anything from her father.

"Our futures aren't set, but with faith will become reality."

She held the scrap up to the screen and tried the call again. The signal wasn't terminated, but the video on the receiving end remained blank. After a few moments, a nervous whisper broke the silence.

"What're you doing? This isn't a secure channel!"

"It's Charista, Joanna."

Joanna's worried face appeared on-screen. "What's going on? Has something happened to Findlay?"

"Something's happened alright."

Joanna's brow creased. "I don't understand. Charista, where is your father?"

"I need to know," Charista began, her voice with a deep tremble, "what made him kill my mother."

Joanna's face twisted in sorrow. Tears streamed down as she lowered her head. "He finally told you."

Charista's own tears blurred her vision. She blinked them away as the tightness in her stomach locked her in position. "I don't understand how he could've done such a thing."

Joanna sighed. "Sweetheart—"

"Don't call me that. You're not my mother." Charista flexed her gut, but she knew the quaver in her voice still showed through. Charista took several hurried breaths as she watched Joanna's pained expression.

Joanna nodded slowly and said, "I never intended to be. Findlay, your father loved your mother. You must realize he wasn't given a choice in what happened to her. Your mother tried to stop Zakmar, to keep him from risking more Omegan lives, but he was too powerful."

Charista swiped her eyes. "But why would Findlay agree to do that?"

"Because Emperor Zakmar threatened to kill you if he didn't."

Charista froze.

"Your parents always wanted the best for you, and when it came down to Winola's life or yours, it wasn't even a choice for either of them." Joanna winced, a compassionate smile on her lips. "Your father has been tormented by this every day since it happened. I know you're hurt and don't want to believe this could've happened. But it has. You must know how broken up he's been. Where are you now?"

"The Omegan Military facility."

Joanna's eyes widened. "You've got to be more careful! This call is probably monitored. We should disconnect. Please don't hold this over your father; he's more broken up about this than you can possibly imagine. Take care of yourself. I'll contact you in time, when I feel it's safe."

Charista nodded and terminated the call. She bowed her head and cried once again. Even though she knew more about the situation, it hadn't healed the pain of her mother's death or what her father did. At least she had more perspective on the situation: that both her parents had acted with her safety and future in mind. She made a silent promise to herself, on the realm of a military oath of service, that Zakmar one day knew her retribution in full.

## Chapter 8

A FTER HER CONVERSATION WITH JOANNA, Charista returned the following day to her family dwelling. It was soon to be her former home, but it already felt alien to her. Findlay was at the table where she had left him, hunched over and asleep. She took a seat across from him. As she sat, he awoke and, after a few moments of bewildered glancing, he focused on her.

"I ran as hard as I've ever run. I cried as hard as I've ever cried. I tried to figure out why this happened, but I know there's no answer and never will be. But I know also, that Mom wanted the best for me."

Findlay watched his daughter with sad eyes, reddened with emotion. He still searched for words.

Charista continued, "I can't understand what possessed you. But you were protecting me. You and mom were protecting me. I don't know if I can forgive you for this. But I also know even more what is driving all this. And I can make you pay, but if I get Zakmar, that brings all this to a resolution. A balance of retribution, anyway."

Findlay nodded as the tears cascaded from his face.

Charista went on. "Our place here was the doing of Zakmar. He put us in this position. I'm going to get myself in power one day, and the Omegans will know us; they'll know what it means to cast aside the Mantiswords. I'll do whatever I need to avenge my mother and you."

Findlay sighed. "I've tried to think of anything to help our situation, but I don't see any way out of this. Zakmar is ruthless. I saw him slaughter a decorated Omegan officer just for what happened at the Omegan outpost on Bertold system. If he learns what I've been doing with Joanna, he'll likely kill you and me. Everything we've built toward would be lost."

In Charista's abundance of fear and emotions, an idea presented itself to her. "What if I turned you in, Dad?"

Findlay blinked for a few moments.

Charista, the idea taking more root in her mind, straightened herself up. "You said it yourself, we're likely both dead. But you've planted seeds with Joanna, and if she carries on what you've started away from watchful eyes, we still have a chance."

Charista noted the wistful, pained look on Findlay's face. While all his cycles of thorough planning and calculations hadn't prepared himself for this moment, the love for his daughter and the chance for her survival made her plan seem not only plausible, but even necessary.

"If that's what it will take for you to survive, then let's do it." Findlay's body sank lower into his seat once he'd said the words.

Findlay reached for Charista, but she felt an odd distance at that point. She smiled but felt herself reserved from her usual return of affection. "There will be a time when we'll be avenged."

## Chapter 9

F INDLAY AND CHARISTA'S PLAN AGREED
upon, the next several days passed in quick fashion.
Findlay reached out to the Railen, and after a lengthy
conversation with Ander Pimm and the continued threat of
disruption in supply, Ander agreed to let Charista be the broker
of their arrangement. The supplies of Brescar to the Railen
would continue under the guise of disposal of Omegana refuse
in Ling Galaxy, a regular process.

Findlay and Charista knew, while their next move was
painful, was a necessary step in their ultimate plan. Charista
contacted Omegana security and Commander Patrach, and
announced the defection of her father. The news was taken with
outward shock. Patrach's anger at the infraction was so serious
that he initially incarcerated both Charista and Findlay, holding
them separately to determine the depth of the transgressions.

They endured a series of tortures, the deepest and most severe that Omegana had developed. The scientific minds offered something in the way of these devices, but the military honed and brought these horrible treatments to a very brutal application.

After nearly a month of isolation and treatments, the Omegans were satisfied that Charista hadn't the ability to have partaken in the transgressions. Charista credited her surviving the torture to her extensive training and Winola's strength in her genes.

Charista knew, as much as she'd physically survived, her mental losses were unrecoverable. The betrayal of her father was a scar on her being, never to be healed, or even covered over by how many cycles passed. She knew her only path was forward, working herself as much as she could into the Omegan military machine until, one day, she was able to exact the revenge she fully knew Omegana deserved.

Commander Patrach visited Charista as she was in a medical facility, recovering from the last rounds of her interrogation, aka torture. She lay in a bed, connected to several tubes that supplied her body with fluids. Once she caught sight of Patrach, her mouth formed a line. She attempted a salute until the soreness in her body made her stop.

"Rest easy," Patrach said. "You're acquitted of the charges. Your father will be sent for execution in short time. The fact you turned him in is your saving grace in this matter."

Charista managed a nod in reply.

"I know the treatment makes talking difficult, so I'll forget the customary respect given to Omegan military leaders. You have a hard road ahead, Charista Mantisword. You must earn my trust. After all, your parents did to ruin my good thoughts of the Mantisword name. Rest assured, I'll be watching you closer than any other graduate."

Charista tensed. She nodded again while her insides screamed for her to lunge for Patrach's throat.

Patrach continued. "Now then, you'll be assigned to a menial detail at first; pardon me if my trust is a little harder to earn. I pride myself on military loyalty. Don't worry. Do your time in your first assignment, keep your mouth shut and follow orders, and you'll find your way moving to more challenging posts when you've proven yourself in my eyes."

Charista nodded. She knew the game was Patrach's and Zakmar's for the time being, but with her getting on board, the situation would one day be hers to control.

Findlay's execution was broadcast as he'd predicted. Seated facing the screen, he wasn't given any chance at speaking a final penance. Zakmar had already ordered a close watch on Charista while her initial assignment would be ensconced heavily around a group of avowed Omegan loyalists. Zakmar demanded regular reports on Charista's activities from Patrach. Her treatment wasn't an official probation, but it may as well have been.

Charista stood in a room with fellow Omegan military as they watched Findlay receive the toxic inoculations that would swiftly take his life. There would come a time for Patrach and Zakmar; they'd all suffer dearly.

The injections took a few minutes to take hold. Charista glanced away from her spot at the far end of the room. She dabbed the moisture from her eyes as she watched the life of this Omegan who loved her more than anything slip from her. She felt the death she watched on-screen filter to her, as part of her very essence atrophied and died. Charista mourned for three people in that moment: her mother, who'd she'd just slightly known, and her father, who'd raised her from a scared youth without a mother.  Finally, Charista mourned who she once was and would never be again: a bright and youthful Omegan female, full of hope with a promising future.

But as a scar formed over all wounds, Charista's hatred and promise of payback grew in place of the final departure of her father.

## Chapter 10

THE OMEGAN CAMPAIGN CONTINUED on, and their reach began to bleed into other quadrants of the Galaxy. The UA policy of sanctions hadn't slowed Zakmar down, and as a response, the UA decided to ramp their restrictions up to a new level.

Once the Omegan reach extended past their quadrant into the more central and higher populated portions of Ling Galaxy, the UA realized their diplomatic measures were pointless and the Omegans were only going to respond to stiff penalties, if anything at all.

The UA made their last attempt at negotiations as Zakmar gathered his leaders for another meeting. Zakmar was reviewing the effectiveness of new weaponry when the comm channel hailed with a message from the UA. Zakmar frowned a bit at the interruption, but decided to entertain the UA. He figured having roused their attention enough for a call was itself a victory for him.

Zakmar sneered at the image of Nic Sava on his screen.

"Yes, Mr. President?"

"Emperor Zakmar, the moves of Omegana are in violation of your treaty with the Universal Alliance. You never had authorization for your activities on the world of Kantit. The mining you've begun there is illegal, and this is your first and only warning to desist these activities immediately."

Zakmar glanced at his group about him. Silencing the audio on the channel back to Nic Sava, he muttered, "Note the phony bureaucrats, how they tremble when they see their feeble hold on order slip away. I think it's time we show these wretched the true power of our race and just what we're willing to do to make our rule over Ling Galaxy a reality."

Zakmar turned back to the screen smugly. "My dear President Sava, I'm sure I don't share your concern over the issues you speak of on the Kantit system. My people are proceeding on their course with no other concern. I advise you to not disrupt them or you'll be answering to my military posthaste."

"This is not a discussion and definitely not a trial, Zakmar. Ellene Ballo and the Nara are in full agreement with the UA on this. Your aggression threatens the very existence of peaceful life in Ling Galaxy; and as such, we are enforcing the most stringent sanctions in UA History on Omegana. Trade to and from your world is suspended. And travel will be most carefully monitored and recorded. Any suspicious activity taking place off world by the hands of Omegans will be treated as an act of war."

"President Sava, you can bottle us up, but what are you thinking about our exploits on the Tausian system?" With that, Zakmar activated a display visible to those in the room with Zakmar and to Sava himself. Tausian, a metropolitan city, was displayed. Shimmering tall buildings hosted an array of beings working while a slew of small craft wound around the buildings in a continual stream of commerce on the system. Suddenly, a group of Omegan craft burst onto the scene, firing on various targets, causing chaos and destruction as billows of smoke burst forth from several locations.

Sava froze, his scowl deepening. "You'll pay for this, Zakmar! As sure as I breathe, you'll regret this."

"I'm sure I will." Zakmar deactivated the screen and turned back to his group. Their tense faces weren't as affirmative as he'd liked, so he added, "We're Omegans; never forget. We've survived centuries of servitude, of being ordered, of worker status, but now we are ready for our rise.

"We are not a treaty!" Zakmar slammed his fist on the table, which made others in the room, especially the Science team members, flinch. Even Commander Chun jerked back slightly in surprise. "We'll never succumb to the law of the Universal Alliance. We are meant for more, deserve more, and one day we will have more. No one, not the Railen, not the Xeno, or any living beings in Ling Galaxy, not even the Nara, will have their say over what we do or who we are!"

The discussion was stopped immediately when a super-brilliant burst of light flashed in the center of the room along with a tremendously loud popping noise. Once their eyes adjusted, they noticed on the table stood a female. She was dressed in ceremonial robes including a hood that covered her face. But her scaly black skin and glowing yellow eyes weren't hidden, and she uttered a series of hisses.

In reflex, Patrach and Chun drew their weapons while members of the Omegana Science Wing edged themselves further under the table.

Zakmar was more curious than concerned and stood. "How the hell did you get in here? This is a private council. State your business before we terminate you."

The hooded figure said nothing, but strode about the narrow platform for a few moments. They then uttered more guttural noises—part gurgles, part hisses. Zakmar eyed Patrach and Chun, their weapons trained on their mysterious guest, waiting for the nod from their emperor to shower the stranger with a lethal barrage.

Zakmar was just about to order their fire when their guest spoke. "I bring a message from Malone Stanton, heir apparent to the throne of Ling Galaxy."

"Ling isn't a kingdom, but since you bring it up, the only ones who'll get that seat are Omegan blood. Consider that my message to Malone."

The hooded figure snapped to, her eyes in line with Zakmar. "Tyrants will tremble, rulers will relent, the strong will suffer. Service to Malone is your alternative to death."

Zakmar's next glance to Patrach and Chun was enough of a word. The air was sliced with the sound of weapon fire, but as Zakmar focused on their target, he felt a sharp pain in his chest. He grabbed for the area and pulled his hand back to see it covered with greyish Omegan blood.

The figure vanished from the room as quickly as it had entered. Seconds later, the sounds of groaning from the rest in the room filled the silence.

"Multiple wounded!" Patrach called into the comm from the room. "Send medical. Emperor Zakmar among the victims."

## Chapter 11

THE STRANGE VISITOR WAS MORE INTERESTED with shock and awe, and a few minor injuries, including some lacerations to Zakmar himself. Once the confusion was resolved and the wounded including Zakmar were treated, Zakmar ordered a meeting with the Omegan Science team, as well as leaders from his Military Wing. He wanted a reasoned approach before more brute force. There was certainly time for bludgeoning, but Zakmar decided for the moment on a more practiced approach.

Chun spoke first. "The Looker transported to our place. We've been aware of their capabilities for some time now. The Nara had issued warnings on them and, in particular, Malone Stanton. He's ruthless and out for control of Ling. Some way or another, our path will bring us up against him, and it appears to have just happened."

Zakmar scoffed at Chun's take. "Of course, I know this. Tell me what can we do to protect ourselves from this kind of attack again."

"Not much, I'm afraid," Patrach replied. "His Lookers make runs as they want. They travel dimensionally; we don't yet have a way of stopping them. As an alternative, I advise we look a different way, in incorporating that design."

Zakmar froze. "Are you suggesting we join with them?"

"Only if it serves our interests." Patrach cautioned.

Chun grunted his agreement, adding, "Malone has apparently figured out a way to harness Essence. I don't think he's merged with it yet; we would've heard about that. Still and all, the dimension shifting abilities and threat that poses worries me. We don't want to face Malone if he does successfully merge with Essence. Let's divert some strength to that issue. We need to get on top of this problem before something like this last attack happens again. We can't have anyone standing in our way."

Patrach and others in the Omegan military offered support for Chun's suggestion, but Zakmar paused with the practiced air of someone who'd made his way to power as he had done.

Zakmar said, "Malone is a bastard, plain and simple. However, we must remember to be resourceful. I have no doubt of our strength, and when the time comes in a straight-out fight, there's none in Ling Galaxy who can match us. But we sometimes must work smarter too. Malone has a decided advantage with Essence and, for now, I'd rather work with him and help our position in Ling Galaxy get stronger."

"But why would Malone even consider working with us?" asked Patrach. "He doesn't seem to think he needs help from anyone."

Zakmar said, "We need to reason with Malone, let him see that his goals of domination can be met faster with us."

"But what then? We subject ourselves to another life of slavery, serving another master?" Patrach countered.

Zakmar said, "It will have to appear as such, for a while. Our move will be to strengthen our position and eventually overcome him." He turned to the Omegan Science team members, their group still reorganizing in the wake of Findlay's loss. "I'm counting on you to get in with his people, study their ways, figure out what we need to do to replicate their abilities. When the time comes, we'll dispatch Malone."

Zakmar's assembled group remained silent. They shared concern about his reaches, but they had to admit his ability at getting the attention and agitation of the UA was unlike any leader they had ever had. Their course forward would include more battles, but with their military strength they carried the Omegan attitude that their cause had only two options: victory or death.

# Chapter 12

THE UA WASN'T AS EASY TO BRUSH ASIDE as Zakmar had assumed. Within a few days, the UA fleet sealed off several transit routes to and from Omegana, choking the resources of the Omegans. Their fuel cell reserves were enough to hold them for a bit, but the upper authorities knew it was just a matter of time before their supply of fuel would be a big concern.

The Omegan move to conquer Ling had temporarily taken a back seat to runs to keep their own people from starving. Food supplies were restricted, and the UA did all they could to squeeze the Omegans into compliance as much as possible.

Zakmar decided Malone was at least a necessity for the time being, until he at least had the upper hand on the UA.

However, contacting the Omegans brought one extra nuance with it. Frey, a former Omegan upstart, had fled Omegan society for reasons unknown. His path had taken him on a collection of illicit jobs around Ling Galaxy before he found himself on the arm of Malone Stanton.

Zakmar had known about Frey's new employment. He wasn't aware, however, about Frey's liaison designation until the comm between Omegana and Malone's stronghold was established and Zakmar gazed into the smug expression of one of his former officers.

"Frey, what a surprise."

Frey chuckled for a moment. "That's one word for it, Emperor Zakmar."

Zakmar realized the already rough task of appeasing Malone Stanton was going to be even more painful than he'd thought. "I'm not in the mood for games here and I have nothing to say to a deserter. Connect me to Malone Stanton at once."

Frey's brow creased a bit in response and he offered a slight smile to Zakmar's demand. "I'm afraid you're not speaking with Malone until we discuss your intentions first."

Zakmar's annoyance blossomed into anger quickly. Who the hell was Malone to put up some mealy turncoat as a buffer, anyway? "I don't have time to sift through whatever you've done that got you where you are now, Frey. I want to get a message to Malone Stanton about an opportunity he'll be interested in."

Frey had handled contacts from others around Ling Galaxy that mentioned similar arrangements. Malone's swiftly growing reputation made his unaffiliated status in Ling Galaxy almost as attractive as his potential power over Essence. Unfortunately for Zakmar, Frey had developed quite a shrewd approach to bargaining, and had given Malone enough loyalty to make Frey a definite gatekeeper for access to Malone.

"I'm sure you think that, Zakmar," Frey said. "Before we go further, you'll have to give specifics on what Omegana promises for this arrangement."

"Frey, I'm offering you the services of my numbers, my military."

Frey nodded. "And just what are you expecting in return?"

"Why, the opportunity to serve the great Malone Stanton, of course."

Frey shook his head slowly. "Don't insult my intelligence like that. Tell me, what are you looking for?"

"We want access to Essence as well. We want to learn your ways. There's no reason we can't both benefit from Malone's power."

"Knowing the ways of Essence is more than just physical purity. It's a continual search for the truth at the heart of existence."

Zakmar nodded. "We've got the strength, Frey. You know we do."

Zakmar's discussions continued with Frey, part of the necessary dance for entre into partnership with Malone. Zakmar flexed every bit of his diplomatic muscle in the negotiations that followed, while keeping one eye on the coup of Malone he knew would one day come.

## Chapter 13

CHARISTA'S ASSIGNMENT WAS HANDED DOWN very much like a prison sentence, and the nature of the job wasn't too far off from one. Given her father's offense, her assignment was changed accordingly. From her former post with the Omegan infantry in the Horde, she was moved to the most rear of echelons possible. The refabrication service of Omegana hadn't so much as claimed the honor of least glamourous Omegan assignment. Rather, the depot was assigned that title due to lack of any other occupation claiming a worse status among the hierarchy of Omegana.

The outpost wasn't even on Omegana proper. On a distant moon of the Omegana system, the refabrication plant sat in the middle of acres of scrap: crashed starcraft, mangled weaponry, both personal size and extra-large in-ground fixed varieties. All pieces in this chaotic collection shared one common trait—

they'd seen their life in service of Omegana or her enemies and had been rendered useless or broken by one way or another.

Charista realized her placement wasn't just because of how remote it was. She too, like her parents before her, was deemed broken, unfit for regular Omegan service. But she knew there wasn't anything further from the truth, and the day would come that she'd prove that assessment wrong and take her place ruling Omegana from Zakmar himself.

Charista eyed the work area before her, covered with damaged pieces of Omegan weaponry and craft. Over the tables hovered a series of tools and equipment for repair. Her initial assignment involved the maintenance of Omegan hardware damaged in battle for its return. It was a far cry from the glorified battlefronts the Omegans fought on, but it was a necessary and minor department of their military complex. Not to mention, it was a suitable punishment for someone who hadn't quite yet earned her way back into the fold of the trustworthy.

Renfrid Speck, Charista's supervisor, wasn't humorous by Omegan standards, which was quite a statement. His burly frame was made all the more menacing by the posture he held— shoulders hunched forward and a slight lean toward the front. He'd stepped back from a long career training Omegan military from their initial phase, where Renfrid had the reputation of being as fierce as Zakmar among his top military and scientific leads.

"I'm well aware of your history, probie. And don't think for one Omegan minute I want you here any more than I want my head cut off. Your no-good piece of trash father is worthless space filth, and I'd just as soon see you offed like they did him."

Charista focused on her breathing until it slowed.  She repeated her thought to herself.  She started this not long after Findlay was first sentenced.

*I am alive.  I am OK.  I'll make them pay.*

Those words were the steps she took.  Whenever times were tough, whenever it felt too hopeless for her, whenever the doubt came on and was too big to deny, she repeated those words over and over again.

She knew though that a vow of silence wasn't the way.  Her path to revenge was going to take her through the ugliest parts of herself.  "I'm not proud of what happened.  I can only pledge my loyalty to Omegana."

Renfrid, sensing Charista's discomfort, grinned in enjoyment.  "As long as we're on the same page here.  I never wanted you at this post, and for some reason I'm sure I'll never understand, Zakmar didn't want you killed in kind with your low life papa.  So, do what I tell you, run these rebuilds like I say, don't give me any lip, don't make any mistakes, and I'll see about getting your sorry face out of my facility as soon as I can."

"Fair enough."  Charista tensed again; she knew this path before her was her only one.  But she had her mantra; she repeated it to herself so much she heard it repeat in her mind like a continual echo.

In her free time, Charista studied the monitor in the main console area.  The large screen was their connection to the rest of Ling Galaxy, to Network and, for Charista, her future.  She switched the view on screen to show the off-world perspective, into their immediate quadrant of Ling Galaxy.  She watched the collections of stars, systems, and starcraft that passed through the area steadily.  *One day*, she thought, *this Galaxy will know me. And I'll be the most powerful one in it. I control my own destiny.*

Charista found her way through the main system and the project files until one caught her attention. An alteration process. The Omegans were interested in assimilating into other cultures, including the ability to alter their physical appearances to match those of another race.

Her thoughts were jarred with a sharp slap on her hand and she glanced up into Renfrid's agitated face. "Ay, what are you doing in there? That's got nothing to do with your job." He angrily closed out the screen, and she faced him.

"I'm sorry, I was curious what was going on."

"You aren't here to be curious; you aren't paid to learn. You're here to do whatever I tell you. Remember, this may as well be a dead end for you, far as I care. Don't give me any reason to worry. That's all you gotta think about, got it?"

Charista offered a quick nod. She wondered what would happen to her if she attacked Renfrid. He was big but slow. She could've at least gotten a few good swings on him, maybe even made a run away from the place. But insubordination was bad enough; striking a superior would've been a quick end to her already troubled career.

How many things had changed for her. She thought back to Findlay's words, about making her way up the ladder of Omegan military to be able to make their big coup one day. So much had gone apart from that dream. She felt herself in a constant scramble, with only the hope of coming back to some semblance of revenge by the time everything was over.

## Chapter 14

ZAKMAR CALLED AN ASSEMBLY TO THE main hall of the Omegans. These announcements were usually reserved for big moments, so the general excitement in the room beforehand was pretty noticeable. Already relegated to a level in Omegan society a shade above discarded trash, Charista was allowed to view the event from a screen in the refabrication plant. Renfrid joined her for the viewing. Charista noticed Renfrid seemed more animated than usual. She figured, even for him, this had to be a nice distraction from their typical work grind.

The crowd hushed and Zakmar began. "My people, we stand on the edge of greatness. Our Horde is feared throughout the Galaxy. There aren't any races who dare to stand up to us. We will conquer and defeat all who stand in our way. And now, we have another tool in our collection. We have a deal in place that will guarantee our future to rule Ling Galaxy. We've reached out to Malone Stanton and will form an alliance with him."

The audience hesitated in silence at first, but then rumbling took place of the quiet, a low roar built steadily into a large sound of jeers.

Zakmar raised his arms in an attempt to steady the crowd, but it was useless at first. Finally, he leaned into the mike and bellowed: "Omegana is supreme. Have I ever given you reason to doubt me? Do I not bleed as you? Think like you, feel for you, and am one of your native blood? We emanate from the same wellspring, of Mother Omegana, and we are not different. I'd not cut my hand off, not sever my leg or my head. Then why would you ever think I'd make some agreement that would visit harm upon my blood brothers and sisters?

"Malone Stanton will lead us to our goal. We will join with him, not because we believe in him, but we believe in what he will bring to us. We fully intend on conquest of Ling, and we will handle Malone in our way and in our time. Trust me, my faithful. We must take this step to get to our ultimate goal. Believe in me, believe in yourselves, and believe in the future of Omegana!"

Charista noticed Renfrid's enthusiastic gaze gave way to one of shock. Shouts came from the crowd assembled before Zakmar. "He's a maniac! He'll betray us!"

Zakmar steadied the crowd. "We hold the upper hand. We've got our legions, our Horde. We have the weapons, the arsenal. All Malone has is a collection of devotees and some dogma. True, he does have the skills of the Lookers, which is why I want to use him. We can go without, but we would have to come up against him; and I'd rather know where my enemies are, instead of being constantly surprised by them."

Charista clenched her fists as a strong desire to kill Zakmar flooded her body. He was so smug and sure of himself and spoke without any care at all, it seemed. His people loved him for it. Omegana always celebrated the bold and the brash, but the thoughtful and resourceful were somehow left behind. Charista knew that's why Findlay never had a chance with them; he even sacrificed Winola in the hopes it would've meant something to his people, but nothing came from it. Other than a break in their family and a loss Charista knew defined every moment of the rest of her life.

She thought about her plan and hadn't any idea of when it would begin, but she knew that it was happening one day or another. She had to wait her time, though. Like her parents before her, she had a part to play, in being a good soldier and daughter of Omegana. She'd show her race proud and, when the time came, she'd make them all pay. Her vengeance would be three-fold: herself, Findlay, and Winola's.

Charista kept silent. She knew she couldn't contradict or shun anything from Zakmar, or Omegana in general, and, even with Renfrid, the rule for her at present was to bide her time. Hers was a dance, a delicate one that looked to be far reaching. Her time was coming, but not for a while. And until then, it was on her to show the most supportive version of herself she knew how.

Malone's booming voice echoed through the hall, silencing the Omegan crowd instantly. His ghastly face appeared, shimmering in holographic bluish brilliance toward the front of the room. Zakmar turned to Malone.

"Thank you, Malone, for standing with us. I think we will show Ling Galaxy just what true order for all will look like."

Malone nodded and added a smirk. "I'm sure we will, Emperor. Omegans, like you, I've been cast away from the Nara, told I was no good. But unlike the Railen, who, like heartbroken children, are scratching back to the door that was closed behind them, I'm looking forward. Ling Galaxy is our home and together we will make it the place it should be. Not with the Nara's help, but through our own efforts. We will make tomorrow the now it should always be."

Zakmar hoped his disgust for Malone wasn't too clear on his face. He had enough to deal with from the hard line Omegans who had plenty of issues with Zakmar's moves in courting Malone. While the Omegans hadn't any avowed policy against Malone, the fact that Malone was largely an unknown, his allegiance being fairly unclear to anyone except himself was part of the problem. Zakmar always looked at problems pragmatically though and, while Malone's brazen threats seemed to work a purpose with his fellow heads of state, Zakmar knew that even the brashest of megalomaniacs needed backing from a nation. The Omegans weren't the only ones with a military who could serve their might on Malone's side. Zakmar knew the sooner they reached out to Malone, the less time another race had to make their own deal with Malone to the Omegans' disadvantage.

Zakmar continued speaking over the crowd that hadn't fully settled back down. "I'm pleased to introduce the part of our arrangement with Malone Stanton. We pledge our military to be at his disposal in his moves to get the Essence he craves. We'll be given our own share of this substance, and as well he'll offer the services of some of his Lookers in the meanwhile.

"Our efforts will be on the offensive. We must keep our pressure up on the Railen. We've hit them hard, and where they live, but don't count them out for one moment. Ander Pimm is a cunning warrior. But we'll use our strengths too: Omegan might, Omegan technology, and the gift of the Lookers."

The air shuddered for a moment, and then a Looker appeared beside Zakmar. The crowd gasped at first, then offered shouts and jeers customary to an Omegan not used to anyone else sharing their spotlight or glory. Zakmar quieted the crowd down and stepped closer to the hooded figure.

"Remember, my Omegans, we are allies with the Lookers; this is our agreement with Malone Stanton. And I'm giving this Looker the explicit mission: bring me the head of Ander Pimm!"

The crowd roared in response. Zakmar bathed in their adulation. He wanted more than anything to see Ander Pimm's head. He knew it would be the start of a great collection, slain heads of his enemies. Before long he planned to add Ellene Ballo and Malone Stanton to that number.

The Looker pulled back their hood, revealing a female face. Pale skin was marked with a series of black lines in different patterns. Many Lookers decided on their own facial appearances, tattoos, in respect to their abilities. Their ability to slip across dimensions made them worshiped and feared by some, even considered demonic by those of certain faiths in Ling Galaxy.

"Marelene Webber is one of Malone Stanton's Lookers. We've seen what they can do, and now we'll be using their power as we join forces with Malone Stanton. He wants an army; we want conquest. Together, we will succeed!"

Marelene padded about the platform before she stepped into the crowd. The Omegans nearest her formed a narrow wake as she made her way through the crowd. Zakmar watched from the back in mild amusement. It wasn't important to him that the Omegans and the Looker, or even Malone Stanton, were overly friendly as long as the understanding was in place. The end goal was Zakmar's priority.

Marelene found a challenger in the crowd. An Omegan soldier, in part spurred on by his friends, squared his shoulders off and approached Marelene as the crowd opened up a ring around the two in an impromptu contest. Zakmar made his way into the crowd as the two neared each other. They circled each other, Marelene's eyes glowing, her mouth curled in a hungry snarl. Zakmar worried the fragile detente he'd managed with Malone wasn't going to last very long with this situation, and he had to reclaim the order in the room.

Zakmar grabbed his blade and clanged it loudly against his armor. The particular steel of his blade made a very distinctive ring when struck in this way and the resulting vibration stopped everyone in the room, even Marelene. After a few moments, everyone realized the source of the loud ringing and focused on their leader. Marelene stepped towards him.

"We will work together with the Lookers from Malone. I won't tolerate any dissension. Remember, any Omegan who fails to follow suit with my orders here will be subject to the same treatment as an Omegan deserter."

The Omegans quieted down, and Marelene was more relaxed as a result. She faced the audience. "We start with attacking the Railen fleet and their hidden cache of starcraft not destroyed on the Delfina system. The biggest enemy of the Omegans is our biggest enemy. Together we will hit the UA hard and destroy the remnants of their control over Ling Galaxy. They'll learn they cannot be greater than Omegans. The Lookers and Malone Stanton are with you!"

After a few moments, the screen returned to the Omegana crest. As Charista mulled over what she'd seen, Renfrid slapped his thighs. "OK, then. Back to work, for the glory of Omegana."

Charista held a hand over her mouth when she scoffed out of reflex. *Omegana's dreams and visions aren't the same as mine. But they will be, one day,* she thought. *I'll show them who really runs Omegana, and they'll finally all pay for what they did to me and my family.*

## The Essence Wars Series

All of these titles are available individually on Amazon.com

Xeno Reckoning

Gambit of Dares

Quest for Dominion

Quantum of Destiny

Vengeance Directive

Balance of Retribution

Revenge Nexus

Stratagem Awakening

Collateral Crisis

## Have you read the Valkyrie Chronicles Series?

Forced into a life she hates by the government of Lebabolis, the last human nation on Earth, Ana Crucinal must comply with her pre-ordained future or undergo Realignment. But when her brother falls ill, Ana joins up with the resistance in an attempt to flee Lebabolis—only to learn that the true threat lies elsewhere: an alien race known as the Omegans. All of this was foreseen. A thousand years ago a man living in New Orleans had imagined the future Ana now lives in. He wrote about the resistance, the alien menace, everything. Desperate to save themselves and the remnants of the human race, the resistance formulates a plan to do the only thing they can think of: travel back in time to save the future.

With her enemies closing in, Ana knows this is her one chance to save herself, her brother, and the resistance. Failure is death and the never-ending enslavement of humanity.

Buy the books of the Valkyrie Chronicles Series on Amazon today and find out why so many have fallen in love with Ana and her mission.

## Want a free story?

Destination Exodus is a prequel story I wrote for the Essence Wars series you just read. This story features Erick Ravencraft, father of Selina Ravencraft, as part of the group of humans who leave Earth and the Milky Way galaxy in the hopes of survival. Can they navigate the dangers standing between them and their goal? Go to the following URL to get your free copy! www.paulheingarten.com/email-list/

## The Essence Wars Continue!

The Apostate Progeny, the first FULL LENGTH novel in the Essence Wars Series, is coming soon! Get ready to hear the story of Pierce Sava, son of the current ruler of the Universal Alliance, Nic Sava. Pierce had more than a few disagreements on how things were run, and decided it best he went his own way, in the wilds of Ling Galaxy. Employed by the Syndicates, Pierce is content with his life of running cargoes and mixing it up with his friend Ket Durban. But, when the UA and Nic Sava face a crisis, can Pierce find it within himself to return to the life and the love he left behind, to help the UA restore their crumbling order as the Essence Wars rage on?

## About the Author

Paul Heingarten spreads time between writing, being a musician, and, since 2002, a career in Information Technology. He lives in the southern United States with his wife Andrea.

## Other Titles by Paul Heingarten

The Harvest (short story)
Leave from Absence (novel)
The Monitor (short story)
Natural Election (short story)
Cataclysm Epoch (novel)
Settling Darkness (novel)
Valkyrie Rising (novel)
Menace Ascending (short story)
Xeno Reckoning (novelette)
Gambit of Dares (novelette)
Quest for Dominion (novelette)
Quantum of Destiny (novelette)
Vengeance Directive (novelette)
Balance of Retribution (novelette)
Destination Exodus (short story)
Revenge Nexus (novelette)
Stratagem Awakening (novelette)
Collateral Crisis (novelette)